Meeting People where theyre at The path to something new

JONATHAN QUARTERMAN

Augustina Holmes

MEETING PEOPLE WHERE THEYRE AT THE PATH TO SOMETHING NEW

Contents

TItle

MEETING PEOPLE WHERE THEY'RE AT
THE PATH TO SOMETHING NEW

by Jonathan Quarterman

In loving memory of my two brothers gone but
not forgotten Khrstian Dion Harris and Laithandais
M. Studmire , the inspiration they had on me to
finish this book has finally come true.

Introduction

Meeting people where they're at means – understanding that everyone has their own struggles in life and in order to reach those people you must meet them in that struggle.

Chapter 1

PUT GOD FIRST

If you can make one step God will make two

In life, we are bound to make some mistakes, but those mistakes often arise because we either live in our own way, where no one can tell us anything, or as individuals, we refuse to use the wisdom God has given us to help avoid any type of situation that may bring us harm mentally and spiritually.

As young adults, we try to live our lives the best way possible, knowing that we all have some type of flaws that we deal with daily, but that's a part of life. Without our flaws, we don't really know who we are because we're not perfect, and mistakes will be made to show us who we are. Even though mistakes are a part of life, that doesn't mean we're alone. No matter how hard things may get, just know God is right there by your side, even though you can't physically see Him; He's there. As life moves forward in order to reach our true potential, we must realize that we must put God first because without Him, nothing we do would be possible. So, we must give Him the praise because He's the reason for us waking up in the morning, so God must come first. The reason for putting God first is to know that our success is not just from our hard work and determination but from the grace of God, who has blessed us with the talent and ability to do the things we do every day, whether that be a sport, music, or a passion of ours. Just know it was God-given; we are gifted; we must figure out what our gifts are.

God can open the door to your gift, but it's up to

you to walk through that door. This is why putting God first is so important because no matter what you do in life, He's still rooting for you to walk the path He has set for you. Sometimes we forget that He knows us better than we know ourselves, so it's best we at least try to listen and follow the direction He has provided for us while being mindful of His guidance. We not only figure out what's important but also discern what truly matters. All these thoughts come to mind when putting God first, as He holds paramount importance. By prioritizing Him, questions arise that demand answers. I firmly believe that events in our lives unfold for a reason, yet certain situations can be avoided if we pay heed to the signs God sends us daily. It's our responsibility to listen and observe these signs; neglecting them can lead us into unprepared or unnecessary circumstances which are called test.

When facing tests, God is merely opening us up to something new and better, for progress often requires trials. God possesses a sense of humor, knowing when we're ready or not. Be patient, take your time, and when the test comes, assess your readiness. Always keep Him first, and regardless of the outcome, remain true to yourself. Sometimes, being ourselves is all God desires, fostering a deeper connection with Him. Putting Him first entails understanding there's more for you to accomplish on this earth. I genuinely believe that prioritizing God offers clarity, emphasizing the importance of discipline and the principle that to receive, one must give.

Remember, once you give your time and energy to God, observe how things change and manifest in your favor. What is given to Him will be given back; understanding how to put God first is crucial. This involves making God the number one priority in your life and building a relationship. This relationship entails studying His word, reading the Bible to gain a better understanding of who God is and why He's indispensable in your life. As you delve into the depths of God's teachings, your faith will inevitably grow stronger.

Chapter 2

The Process

Every one's journey is different from each other's.

The process is that no matter what you are going through in life, there are going to be trials and tribulations in the beginning. However, understanding that your blessings come with time and patience is crucial. Nothing in life is given to us; everything we do in this life is a challenge. Understanding that failure must take place for you to grasp the essence of life is vital. You are going to have ups and downs, but once you realize that your blessings are around the corner, things will start to look up for you. Understand that God wouldn't put you through anything you couldn't handle.

Failure is nothing to be ashamed of; it's the general notion of understanding that failure is not always a bad thing but can be used as motivation. Most people perceive failure as a loss or disappointment, but just because something didn't go your way doesn't mean you should instantly give up on it. Instead, take that failure and turn it into motivation. Understand that failure is a part of life, and you must know how to respond to it once it has taken place. As people, we often feel that everything is about us, for example: thinking things revolve around you or that things should happen for you and only you. We must keep in mind that someone is always going through something much worse. We must be more thankful for what God has given us. Each step-in life is a process, whether it is to find love or discover your purpose.

The outcome of your life depends on who you are as

a person and the choices you make. No matter what, each of these components is eventual steps to take, not only in life but toward a better version of yourself. When it comes to finding yourself, it's all about discipline – the practice of training to obey rules you have set for yourself – and understanding that it's all about protecting your moral character. Realize you're not a failure and understand that God created you for a reason. It may seem that life is out to get you, but always remember that you're not alone. Before you can truly become successful, you must fail first. This is all a part of God's plan to shape you into the person He wants you to be, not the person you want to be.

When it comes to loving yourself and someone else, you realize how important it is because it takes the most time; each heart is different. God may have made all of us in His image, but He for sure made us different from each other. So, trying to understand who you are may take more time than expected, but you want to be the best version of yourself when God puts that special person in your life. He knows who's for you and who isn't; you must decide whether it's for you or not. Yes, we are all human, and falling for someone can be hard, especially if feelings are not mutual; this means you must realize it's not your time. Sooner or later, God will open that door, and you will know for sure; but for right now, put it in His hands.

When it comes to "the process to your purpose," you must be humble and have a deep serious talk with God. This takes place by opening your heart to

Him and letting Him know how you truly feel. Prayer is the best way to open up, and it yields results. It may not feel right now, but sooner or later, your purpose will begin to reveal itself. Continue to follow the plan God has for your life. Sometimes, waiting is part of the test because God may have things for you that you aren't ready for. You will know when the timing is right, meaning: When everything starts coming together that you have been praying for or wanting badly. You never know what God truly might have for you; it could be a new job, marriage, or even getting closer to Him. Things will start to open in your favor, but you must remember that God will put things in front of you, declaring that in due time everything you're being patient for will come to the full front at the right time. Now it might take some time, but God doesn't make mistakes when it comes to His children.

During this process, you are going to lose people you thought were on your team but were only on your team ultimately for their gain. It's okay to let go of those types of people; it's all a part of God's plan. To understand His plan, you must realize that things may not happen overnight. It takes time, but with time comes growth, and with growth comes new beginnings.

I believe God has a plan for all of us, and I think we all have something special inside of each of us to not only give ourselves but to the world. The world we live in is cruel and unforgiving, but it's up to you if you want to make a change. Just know, it's good to be generally different from everyone else. The life you live is all about the decisions you make and learning how to work with what you have. When it may feel like you don't have much, you may have a lot more than you think. I know that you may get frustrated trying to figure out why everything you do takes so long to come to light. The answer is learning patience and trusting God's timing. It may seem like things are not reachable, but good things come to those who wait. This is all a part of understanding who you are as a person. You must figure out if you're willing to make sacrifices now for something far greater in your future. Learning to sacrifice comes with being humble and knowing that your time is coming. It may not be right at this moment, but God knows where you stand and where you're going. Each task will be more challenging than the last; the reason why things would be more complex is that life isn't fair sometimes, and we all go through certain situations. Each time you think you have overcome something; you're only touching the tip of the iceberg. Any type of situation that bothers you could change your character if you allow it.

What it may take to get through your struggles depends not only on you but the strength of your faith. Regarding your faith, it's connected to your heart and what you believe about things in life. As individuals, we try our best to overcome all types of challenges. The good news is that these challenges can be overcome; you must go about each situation, learn the lesson in it, and trust the process. All in all, your spirit is something special that God created, and without it, you would not be the person you are today. Your spirit is who you truly are inside. Sometimes, it takes a while to find it; but once you do, you will experience pure happiness.

Chapter 3

Baby steps

Life is all about taking your time.

The road to life is about making choices, and those choices start with different types of steps that you may have to take in this journey called life, like baby steps, for instance, understanding the concept of babies and how they walk. It takes time and a lot of patience for a baby to gather enough strength to start walking and taking its first steps, but the key word is patience. As we continue to grow in life, we tend to get a better outlook on life. As humans, we grow and mature in baby steps because we are not ready for what God truly has for us; so, we must start small to handle the bigger blessings. The reason is that when babies are born, they tend to have small hands at first, and it's hard for them to handle items larger than their hands, but they still try even though they can't handle it. It's not until they get older that they will develop larger hands so they can handle all types of items that may come their way.

The way you might look at things, in the beginning, may overwhelm you because you're unsure if following these steps will completely guarantee you success. In a way, it's all about finding out who you really are and wondering if you can be patient enough to take your time becoming the best person you can be. When it comes to baby steps, you must understand that it may take longer to reach your goal, but just know once you reach it, no one will ever tell you that being patient and following God isn't effective.

Taking baby steps can be some of the hardest

times of your life because you're still figuring yourself out and who you are. We use baby steps for so many things, and once we, as individuals, understand its purpose, which means taking your time to understand yourself better, when we are taking baby steps, we move slowly because we do not want to rush things that may take patience.

Once you reach that new step in life, more opportunities will open for you because God sees that you're ready for more blessings. Even if you take the time, it doesn't mean other obstacles won't try to intervene and destroy what God might have for you. So, be mindful of the steps you take because the devil comes to kill, steal, and destroy. Some of those things would be taking your own life, falling into depression, and destroying the relationship you have with your Lord and Savior. The list goes on, but these are just a few things that come to mind.

Each step you take is a lesson because these steps prepare you for the future. You may not be where you want to be, but with time, I'm sure you will find your way. Things always start off small, but with faith and following in God's footsteps, you can achieve greater opportunities that are on the way. Having a relationship with the Lord will reveal the baby steps in your life so you can be prepared to handle the bigger goals God has put in your life for you to achieve. It's time to wake up! I know no one's perfect, but let's try to take these steps before we aspire for a life we are not ready for; it's all about God's timing and learning patience with God. We each take these steps by understanding who we truly are and our purpose. We also take these steps by not being in a rush with life but letting it flow; everything in life starts with patience. Some of the things we can do to help us get there on our journey are to be obedient to God's will, stay focused on the path, learn that your failures are your blessings, not a curse, and finally, take your time. Each step moves us closer to the natural blessings that God has provided for us. So be ready because God's waiting on you to see if you're going to complain about the process that he's placed in front of you. Always remember, there's a time and place for everything that comes your way! We, as humans, always want things to come to us, but we forget that for those things to come, we must put the work in to achieve them. Now the work we must put in could be prayer, putting God first in everything we do, changing our old ways, and not procrastinating our time. It may not seem like a lot, but everyone's work is different; just remember to follow the path God has guided you to.

When it comes to baby steps, they create the pattern for the life God wants us to live; it opens opportunities you never thought were possible. The steps you take toward life now are all preparation because once those certain opportunities appear, you need to be ready. God has a calling over each one of us. Each of our journeys is different, but the steps we take to start off small before we reach where God wants us to be. If you're willing to learn new things and take risks, the risk that takes is learning that you will never know who you truly are until you step out of your comfort zone. Taking a risk is about taking a chance not only on life but yourself. We need to take risks because it opens the door to a better understanding of who God truly made us. Even though life will still be hard, but you will be able to handle the hard situations that come your way because of the risk you took to get there. Sometimes we look for answers, not knowing in this journey called life that you have to be patient with God's timing. You must be willing to take the steps He gives you, no matter how big or small they are.

Chapter 4

Surviving the Climb

No matter what you go through just know giving up is not an option.

Surviving the climb is basically doing what needs to be done so you can make it in this world. This world can be very cruel, and learning how to survive in it may take some time. In life, timing is everything, and it's imperative that we use our time wisely. No matter how hard the climb may be, it's all about moving forward. The climb is the starting point of life, which could be your freshman year of college, high school, or a new job. Each of these starting points is a new beginning that we all encounter in life at some point. Another part of the climb is a course correction, which means there are going to be obstacles along the way that may take you off your journey. But remember, the climb to life is a process. Surviving the climb is understanding that you are going to have ups and downs in life. The stage of the climb is for us to make decisions that will guide us into becoming a better person. God wants you to be the best you can be, but it's up to you!

As we continue with life, we start to understand that mistakes will be made, and we must learn how to adjust and overcome those mistakes. Some things happen for a reason, but don't get discouraged because, in time, all things come together. Surviving the climb is about overcoming obstacles that will stop you from reaching your goal in life. What God might have for you can change your life's outcomes, but you must be obedient. We must realize that everyone's climb is different. Some people climb faster than others, meaning that some people get it early, and others get it later in life. Life can be stressful, and trying to push yourself to become the best you can, it might take some time, but don't be discouraged. Good things come to those who wait. It all starts by understanding who you are. To understand who you are, you must let go of some things that are damaging to you so you can move forward in the direction God wants you to. Sometimes, understanding yourself is just taking a step back from everyone and everything to re-evaluate what you must do to become successful.

At the end of the day, you must make your own path. Your path might not be easy, but anything is possible with dedication and God's guidance. We need to focus on our own path because wherever God is leading us, it will make the climb to success much easier. Be reminded that everyone's path is different from each other; however, we are all trying to reach the same goal, which is to live a successful life. In life, you will deal with all types of situations that your parents or loved ones have not prepared you for, which could be death or rejection, life after college. You must keep a level head through it all so things won't be as diffi-cult, and what I mean is to stay calm within yourself and understand that no matter how hard things get, you must continue to tell yourself you can do it.

You must remember that the devil comes to steal, kill, and destroy, so you must continue to keep God first in your life for you to be successful. So, don't give up on yourself; just stay the course. God has you in His hands, so the rest will follow. Life will only get harder, but without discipline, you won't be able to reach your full potential. For you to reach what's in front of you, things will have to change. There will be bumps and mistakes in the road, but if you're focused on yourself and have God at the center of your life, anything you fight for can be accomplished. It's all about standing firm in what you believe and knowing that God's always in your corner. When it comes to surviving the climb, it takes time and effort, but while you are on that climb, don't forget the journey and all the things you went through so that when you come out on top, you can see how far you have come.

Chapter 5

Reaching a
New You

Becoming the person, you always wanted to be!

Life is all about reaching a point where you feel satisfied and secure in your position. We all strive to reach a point where we don't have to struggle or give up on any dreams we may have. When it comes to reaching a new version of yourself, it's about recreating who you are and who you want to be. Sometimes, we feel the life we are living is meaningless, when, in fact, we are made for something much bigger than we thought. Having faith in God and in yourself can make a significant difference in your life. I know many of you may not be religious, but having a little faith can help you on your journey to becoming a new you.

Remember, faith is believing in oneself that, no matter the circumstances, you have confidence that things will get better. Oftentimes, we forget how important we really are. Wanting to change for the better takes courage because you're telling yourself that the things you are experiencing won't work with the person you are trying to become. Becoming a new you start's from the inside, which is your heart because it's genuine and for a purpose, not because you're tired of being picked on for being who God created you to be. No matter what you do, people will always try to find something in your life to criticize; however, you can change all of that by finding the good in everything you do. Before you can reach a new you, you must first understand yourself. The way to understand yourself is by being completely comfortable in your skin and understanding that your flaws make you who you are. No one is perfect; we all make mistakes. No matter what, always remember that you are not alone and that you have the power to change what you don't like about yourself.

The first step in reaching a new you is letting go of any negative energy or past situations that might be holding you back from reaching your full potential. Some examples of negative energy could be a bad breakup, being fired from your job, or friends and family not believing in you. Each of these things could hold you back if you let them. In order to grow, you must let go of the past and any type of failure that has come along the way. It may take some time to understand the meaning of your failures, but in the end, they are only going to make you stronger and a better person. You will understand that every person who has failed at something has never given up on their dream or themselves. Just imagine where Michael Jordan would be if he had given up because he didn't make the freshmen team. Reaching a new you is about getting rid of the past so you can receive the blessings that God has waiting for you. Some possible ways you can change yourself are to:

1. Never give up on yourself.
2. Don't let your failures define you.
3. Keep God in your corner: meaning keep Him first in your life, because life will get hard at times when you're working on yourself; He's always right on time to guide you through the process.

This road may or may not be easy, but with God's help and the support of family and friends, anything is possible; you just must believe in yourself. When it comes to self-love, you must understand that you matter, and giving up on yourself is not an option. When or if times get rough, you must count on your will to survive and overcome the struggles that lie ahead. It may feel like you're fighting an endless battle, but you're preparing yourself for the future. Change doesn't come just by speaking it, but by having faith and putting forth the effort towards your goal on who you really want to become.

Any type of failure that you come across in your life is to build you up into the person God created you to be. We fail not because we lack the ability or skills, but because we weren't ready for what God intended for us at that point in time. This means you have bettered yourself into the person you want to be. Always remember, good things come to those who are patient. As a religious person, I believe there is a higher power that serves as the head of everything on this Earth. I believe once you realize that the better off you will be, and the reason why is that without God in your life, you won't be able to reach a new you, but with Him, you will be able to do anything you put your mind to.

Chapter 6

PICKING UP THE PIECES

No matter how hard things may get
keep moving forward.

The purpose of picking up the pieces is to understand that everything that has happened in your life is not always your fault. The pieces represent the struggles that you have endured over the past couple of years of your life, they also represent building back up what was broken. Sometimes life throws us curve balls that take our lives on a rollercoaster ride we may not be prepared for. In life, we are all put through a certain amount of trauma, which we all must pick ourselves up from especially if you're going through your situation all alone; but how we pick up the pieces is by building a relationship with God. The devil comes to steal, kill, and destroy whatever God has planned for you. It is important to remember your life matters; just because things are not going your way doesn't mean you're alone in this fight called life.

Your life matters, not only to your family and friends but to God as well. No matter how many times you must pick yourself up, at the end of the day, you're deciding to make a change to better your life instead of letting your failures tear you down. If you know that giving up on yourself is not an option, no matter how hard things may get, know that God is by your side helping pick up the pieces you cannot. In these times, don't lose faith and try to keep your head up because the pieces you're picking up are all connected to your broken heart, trauma, lost faith, etc. Life's not easy all the time and trying to get a grasp on things will only take time because what you're going through cannot be fixed in a day but with time.

You can create opportunities not only for yourself but for a chance to get closer to God. Timing is everything and while you pick up the pieces to overcome your problems, you must be prepared for what lies ahead. This road God has you on is all about being patient and really giving Him your time. Once you understand how to be patient, then you will understand God's timing. Being patient in life is taking things day by day and one step at a time. You cannot get it all in one go you have to work on what you have a be patient for the rest because it's coming. Don't forget to ask God to guide you so He can take His time showing you the path He wants you to take. We feel that we have everything under control mentally, spiritually, and physically, but honestly, we are just holding on to our true feelings. Picking up the pieces is about timing, but also about letting go of anything that may be holding you back from God's gift. We all have a gift, but you must be willing to take a chance on yourself in order to achieve it.

Letting go is a part of the process of picking up the pieces because if you never let go of what's holding you back, you will never be free from it.

So, when it comes to picking up the pieces in your life, it can be anything you've been through in your past or things you are going through right at this moment. No matter what you're going through, don't give up on yourself. Show that faith in yourself can overcome anything that might have had a hold over your life. I'm here to tell you things get better and nothing that is happening to you will last forever. Eventually, you will overcome it if you move forward. It might sound easy, but if you've ever been truly in love, it will not only test your mental strength, but it will test your faith. As you pick up those pieces, you must be willing to forgive anyone that has ever hurt you. God knows you better than you know yourself, so keep pushing and striving for greatness.

Chapter 7

FACE TO FACE

Our greatest battles are the ones within.

"Face-to-face" is coming to terms with the fact that you can be your biggest enemy. The fact that you really don't know yourself also means you have a choice to be yourself. As individuals, we are all afraid to show our true selves, so we put on a mask for people to accept. As individuals, we need to realize that no matter what you're going through in life, there will always come a time when you will have to come face-to-face with your inner self. When you're coming to terms with your inner self, there are some things you will have to deal with on your own. Some of those things may be past trauma or things you have kept to yourself for a long time, but understand that eventually, you're going to have to stand in the mirror. Looking in the mirror causes you to open those closed doors to your life in order to truly find peace.

By coming face-to-face with yourself, you're not only fixing who you are but also understanding the person God created you to be. Sometimes, all God wants you to do is look in the mirror and just focus on the good things and not the bad. The purpose of this method is to help you become a better individual because once you get rid of all the things that were holding you back, like your negativity, you start to re-alize what makes you who you are and notice that life is a blessing and not a curse. Once you learn and real-ize that whatever you're dealing with, God is always in control of your life. You must understand that coming face-to-face with your inner self is important because you have been chosen for greatness. Another reason is the willingness to let go of the baggage that has been keeping you from where God wants to take you. This may open the door for you to see yourself in a different light, whether that be good or bad. The good things are understanding yourself and being appreciative of how God created you. The bad things involve letting the Devil create false information in your head, which makes you want to change what you look like or how you feel about where you are at in life.

As things continue to move forward in your life, you must understand that without struggle and sacrifice, you will never reach your potential. At this point in life, you are still going through the motions, trying to understand who you are and that your inner health plays a big part in your journey called life. When deep down you really don't know yourself, you're stuck trying to keep things together mentally. Because not knowing yourself draws up frustration on who you really are or figuring out "what's so special about me?" In order to figure out who you are, you need to figure out for yourself what matters the most to you!

Dealing with mental health involves things such as depression, anxiety, and even self-love. Depression is something many may encounter in life, either from overthinking a certain situation or a heartbreak. Anxiety is worrying about things you cannot control, which brings frustration. Self-love is caring for yourself for a change and not letting the devil or anyone change who you really are because self-love is the best love. Always remember that in order to love someone else, you must love yourself first. Each of these three mental health issues is just a distraction to take you away from your true path. We were all given a different journey to walk, and you must understand that prayer can help overcome those inner demons.

Remember, you have a choice to look in the mirror and make a difference in your life. The road ahead will be so much easier once you have that one-on-one time with yourself. It's your choice to make a change for your life, and it's up to you because no matter what decision you make, God will still love you the same because He created you. Always remember to never give up on yourself or your dreams. Always know what you're capable of when it comes to yourself. It's all about taking a chance on yourself and not worrying about anybody else. Once you understand that your life is important, then you can move forward.

Chapter 8

WHY ME?

God gives his toughest soldiers the hardest battles.

The life we live is full of surprises, some good and some bad, but there comes a point in each of our lives where we feel enough is enough. So, we tend to ask God why we go through certain things that don't bring us happiness, and sometimes the answer we receive is the type of answer we don't want to hear, so in our defense, we ask questions. The reason you're asking, "Why me?" is because something in your life has transpired in a way you're not used to and you're wondering how this could happen to me when all you do is try to follow your own path or the one God has provided for you since you were put on this earth.

"Why me?" comes from dealing with your inner thoughts that you may feel your life is not where you want it to be at that specific moment. You feel like everything you do is just falling apart because you're not sure where you're truly going in life. So, by the end of each day, we all are trying to come to an understanding that some things happen for a reason and some things happen to help remove you from a certain situation that wasn't meant for you in the first place. I know it's not a good question to ask God, but there comes a time when you need to know if you are being tested. The reason you could be tested is to show us that whatever you are going through, to never give up hope and continue to strive even through the struggle. It can be frustrating at times and there are times you might feel like giving up, but always remember that God wouldn't put you through a storm if he knew you couldn't handle it. So, while you're saying, "Why me?", God is saying "Why not you?" because since he created you, he knows what you're capable of even if you don't see it yourself. God knows what you need and not what you want. Once you begin to understand who you really are and how important your life really is.

After you figure things out, it's time to move forward, especially when your mind is constantly racing and stuck on things that shouldn't matter. The main thing that matters the most is your life. You must realize that your "why me?" stage is only preparing you for the future God has for you. It may take some time at first, but I'm sure things will start to change for the better. You will soon realize that this part of your life will give you a better understanding of what type of person God created you to be and the person you really want to be. Life is all about taking charge of what's in front of you, because eventually the things you thought were your weakness, have become your strength. This is why you're given the "Why me?" test because it helps you see who you are and how far you have come. I know you might that we shouldn't endure the things we go through daily, but without those things, we would not have been able to grow and mature into the person we always knew we could be. So don't ever give up on yourself. Always know that you're important to this world and remember to leave a mark, no matter how small it may be.

Chapter 9

Sacrifice

Sometimes you must give up somethings
to get what you truly want.

Sacrifice is something that enters our lives with the intention of making us better individuals, and it will even change our mindset on how we view life. Giving up on something you love will help transform the person you used to be into someone entirely different. We all must sacrifice something to reach success, but it's also about reaching a new individual version of yourself because there may come a time when people close to you won't understand your actions. Sacrifice is all about giving up on something valued for the sake of something else that you may not understand in the beginning, but in the end, it will all make sense.

People are not meant to understand what God has for them. You may lose friends and even family, but you must understand what's important in your life and who comes first. It's crazy, but God will have you sacrifice the one thing you love the most just to get closer to Him. As you follow in His footsteps, He will guide you toward your dreams and even your goals. Just be patient because your success is right around the corner.

Some of the hardest decisions in life will take some type of sacrifice because we're all trying to make it in this world that we live in. But the question is, are you willing to give up the things you love the most to be successful? We may hear people say that we will do anything to reach our dreams and goals, but when God asks you to sacrifice the things you love the most, will you hesitate or follow through? Don't hold yourself back from what God has for you just because you're afraid to take a leap of faith. You must understand that taking a leap of faith is all about believing in yourself, so no matter how hard things get, it's continuing to move forward and focus on your blessing. Sacrificing something you love to become a better you must start with a relationship with God and knowing that you must trust Him even if you're not sure yourself.

We all have a choice in this life; some may say that sacrificing something that matters to you is pointless, but you must understand that sometimes you have to let go of certain things to receive what's being put in front of you. God just wants the best for you, as you should want the best for yourself. You must understand that we were all blessed with a gift from God, and for us to obtain that gift, we must be willing to sacrifice and die to ourselves. It may take some time, but it will be worth it in the end. Just be patient and watch how God works. Always remember that you have the potential to do anything you put your mind to. So, continue to reach for your dreams and goals.

Sometimes giving something up to reach those goals and dreams will be well worth it. Although it may not seem that way at first, you must understand that every hero you have read about or watched had to sacrifice something to become one of the greats. Even after they're gone, they are still remembered for what they did. So, remember that life is not about settling and being comfortable, knowing that God created you for a specific reason, which is to do His work by following in His footsteps. Another reason is to reach your true potential, which will take sacrifice and even your time. The more you sacrifice, the more you will start to understand why you have dedicated your time and life to something that will eventually bring you happiness. True happiness is being able to obtain your dream or goal and follow through completely.

Chapter 10

Follow your own Path

Sometimes being yourself is all you need!

In today's society, we are so focused on everyone's growth that we often forget about our own. We frequently worry about everyone else's well-being, forgetting whose well-being matters the most. As society grows more and more, the reality is that everyone follows close trends and styles. This will either help you with your social growth or help you reach a certain status for others to notice who you are. But the real goal in life is not to follow the trend but to build your own brand for the present and the future. In life, you must realize that you cannot follow someone else's dreams and goals to become successful. It must be understood that you must follow first and then lead, so in order to grow, you must follow a plan that's not your own first.

once you reach a certain point in your life where you feel comfortable, it's time to move forward and follow your own path. As people, we often have a hard time understanding that real growth comes from our own work ethic and desires. At some point in your life, you must follow the path that was destined for you and only you. Once you realize that, you must continue to follow your own path, and your life will begin to change. As individuals, we must understand that it's okay to be different because following your own path takes courage and a leap of faith that may open doors to new opportunities.

Most people may think that following your own path is only about growth, goals, and dreams, which it is, but it's about making a statement that it's okay to be what God created you to be. Don't ever be afraid to follow your heart. In the process, you may lose friends and even family members, which might mean they weren't supposed to be a part of your journey or their season for time with you has been completed. Things may seem hard at first, but in order to grow, you must give yourself a chance to see your progress. As a society, we often turn our focus toward things that end up being a waste of our time and then wonder why things don't work out the way we want them to. The reason why things don't work out is that your focus is not on yourself but on everyone else, which is causing things to shift in your life.

We must remember that we were all created differently, and if God wanted you to be someone else, He would have made you into someone else. But He didn't because He knew what He put inside of you would cause you to walk a different path. Realize that we are all intelligent in some way or form, and it's up to us as individuals to figure out where we stand in our society and where we are going in life because we all could move forward and make something of ourselves. You took what you had and made the best of it, no matter if you failed or not. Remember God doesn't make any mistakes when it comes to your journey. Your path is your path from the time we are born to the day we die.

God has already predestined your path for you. So, your path is already created; you just must walk it, and that may be the hardest thing to do. As we are walking in life, there will be bumps in the road known as distractions. Distractions thrown your way such as (drugs, sex, and even money) could play a role in stopping you from the path that God has destined for you. In case you didn't realize, the Devil comes to steal, kill, and destroy, which means he will do anything in his power to distract you from your true path and purpose. So, it's up to you to push forward, meaning taking each day step by step and understanding it's not a race to success; it's a marathon. So, in the end, don't forget to follow God and your dreams because they are important to your life.

Chapter 11

Know Your Worth

Just because it looks good doesn't
mean it's good for you.

Life is what you make it, but without knowing your worth, you may tend to let people and certain situations take control of your life without permission. When it comes to knowing your worth, although it may not be easy, you must completely understand who you are and what you stand for. In order to be sure of who you are, you must eventually reach your true self by letting go of the past and the things that have hindered you from knowing your true worth. Always remember that sometimes things aren't what they seem, and you must understand how important it is for you to understand self-worth. Your worth is based on knowing who you are and understanding that just because someone doesn't see what you have to offer doesn't mean you're not important or your worth is not noticed. It just means they didn't value your worth or just couldn't see it.

Over time, your worth will get tested. People will come into your life to use you for your worth because it heals them from any pain, only to leave you all alone after they've gotten everything, they need from you. In the end, it's up to you if you want to give up on yourself or continue to let people walk all over you. So, in this type of situation, you must know that sometimes walking away from a situation will not only help you out individually, but it will also help you see who's really for you and who's not. Remember, life is what you make it, but you must also realize that no matter how hard things may get in your lifetime, know there's a light at the end of the tunnel. Always know that hard work to keep your worth contained does not go unpunished because sooner or later someone will take your worth and amplify it by showing you and your worth matter. Remember, no matter what you go through, good or bad, God makes no mistakes. God made us all different, but he also made us be patient with whatever is in front of us and know that everything that brings you true happiness takes time to manifest.

As individuals, we wake up each day trying to get a better understanding of our worth. We wonder what we should focus on the most. The belief is that people who show their worth to other people are genuinely there to help. So, it is important to remember how important your worth is, and it is important to think about who you allow access into your life. Although things may not always go your way, you are encouraged to stay dedicated to who you are and follow your own path. When you choose to do this, you will not only understand your worth, but you will reach true happiness.

The aim of this book is to capture the attention of those who have experienced similar challenges to mine. I'm not a psychologist, pastor, or counselor; I'm simply a person sharing the trials and tribulations we all face each and every day. Many people are afraid to reveal what we all go through on a daily basis, but this book will reveal what goes on behind closed doors. This inspiration originated from my morning prayers that I used to write in college, and it led me to write this book to assist others like myself.

Jonathan Quarterman